P9-ASC-944

THE NATIVITY

ILLUSTRATED BY JULIE VIVAS

VOYAGER BOOKS • HARCOURT, INC.

Orlando Austin New York San Diego Toronto London

IN THE DAYS OF HEROD THE KING, the Angel Gabriel was sent from God to the city of Nazareth. To a virgin espoused to a man whose name was Joseph, and the virgin's name was Mary.

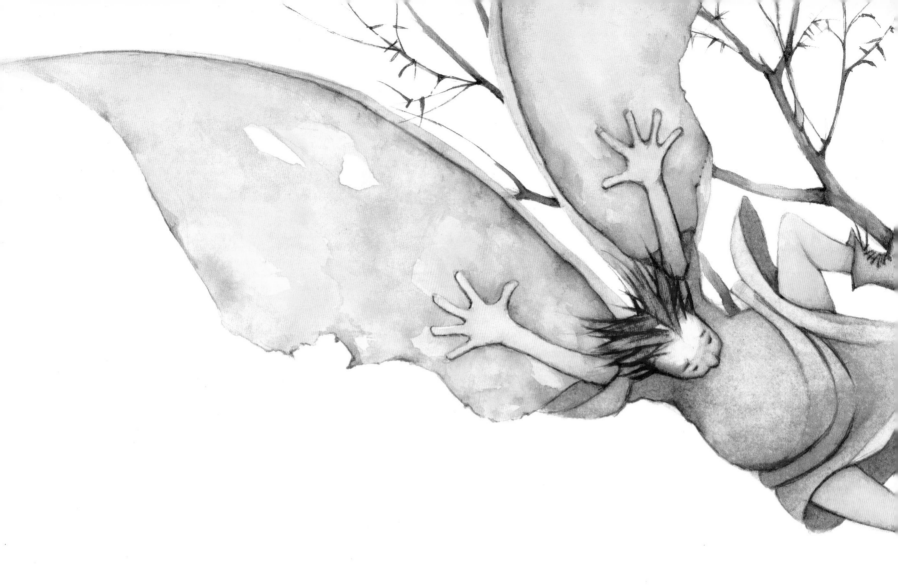

And the Angel said unto her "Hail! the Lord
is with thee. Blessed art thou among women."
And when she saw him she was troubled.

The Angel said, "Fear not Mary: for thou hast found favor with God. Thou shalt bring forth a son and call his name Jesus."

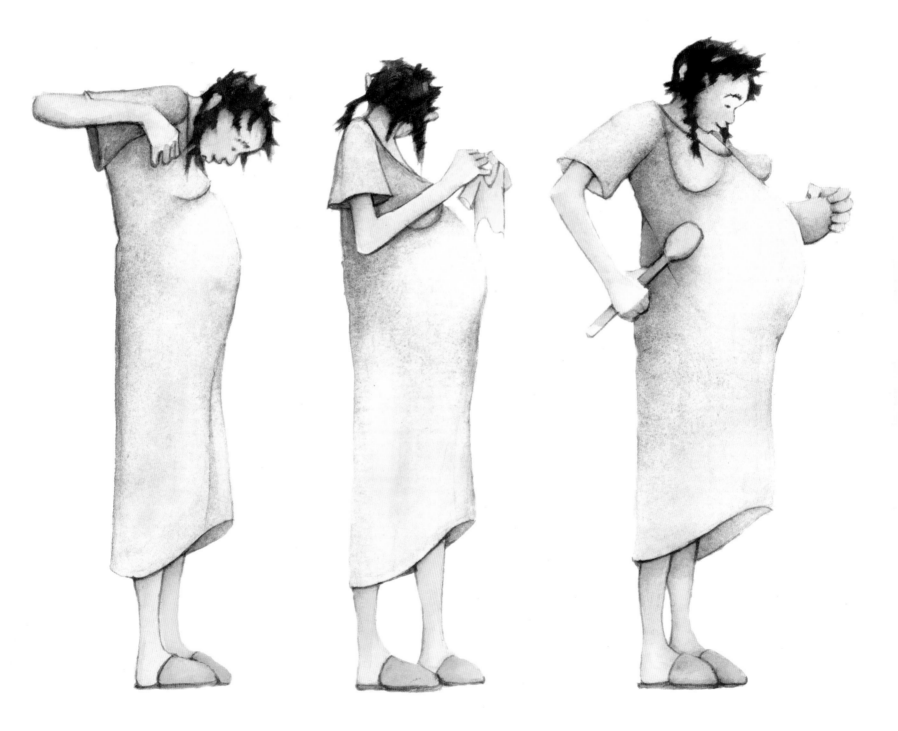

It came to pass that Caesar Augustus decreed that all the world should be taxed, everyone to his own city.

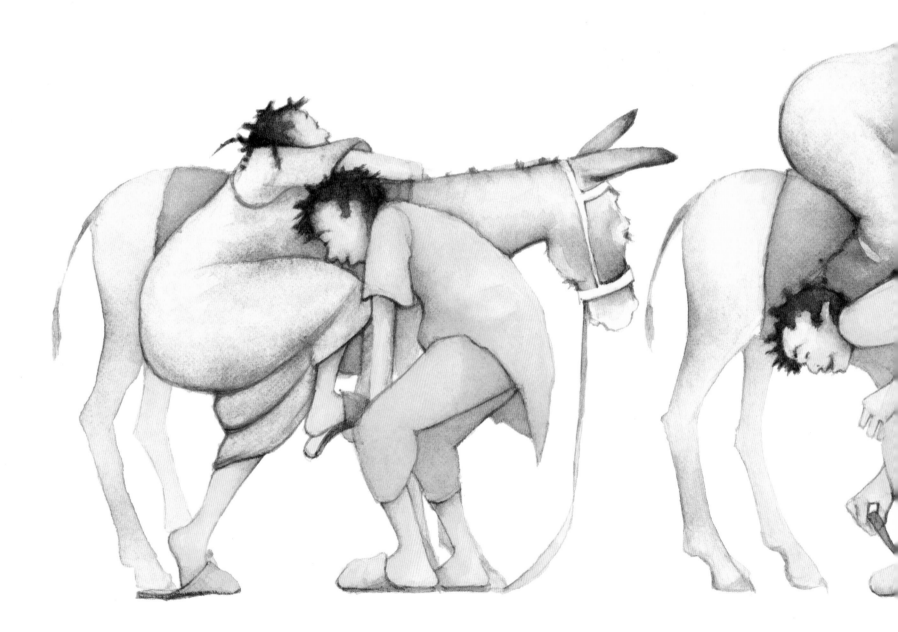

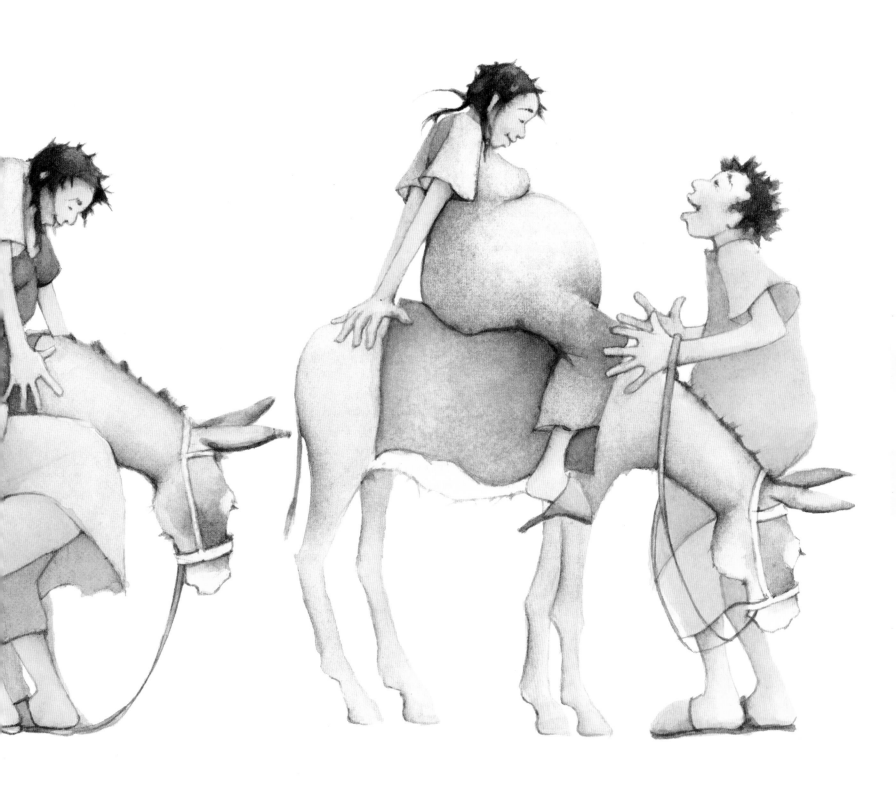

So Joseph went from Nazareth to the city of Bethlehem,
with Mary his wife being great with child.

And so it was that, while they were there,

the day came that she should be delivered.

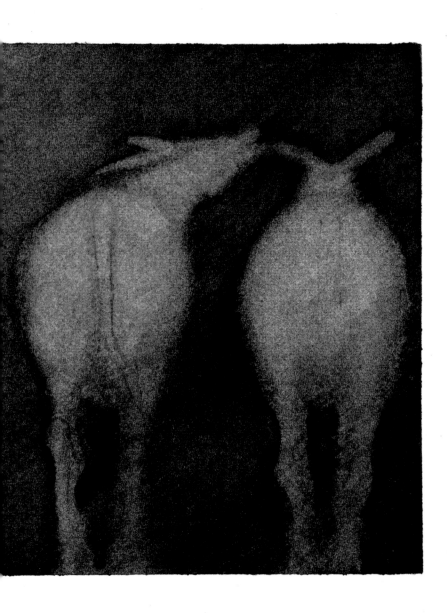

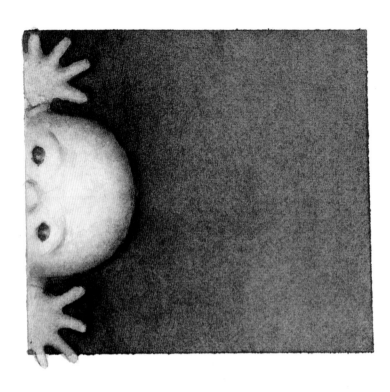

And she brought forth her firstborn son

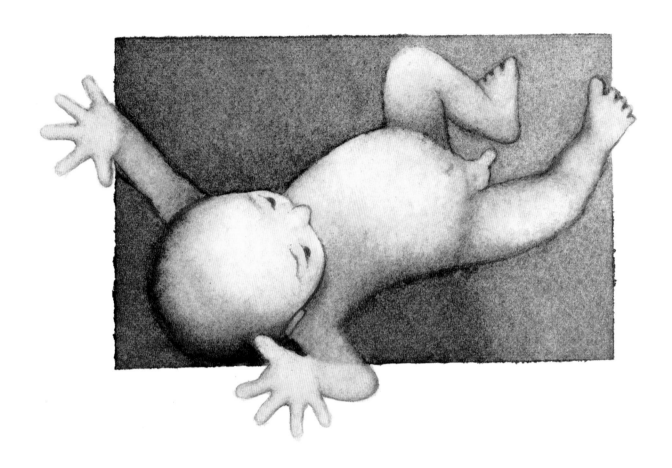

and wrapped him in swaddling clothes, and laid him in a manger, because there was no room for them in the inn.

There were in the same country shepherds in the field, keeping watch over their flock by night.

When, lo, the Angel of the Lord came upon them and the glory of the Lord shone around them and they were sore afraid.

And the Angel said, "Fear not, for I bring you tidings of great joy. For unto you is born this day in the city of David a Savior, which is Christ the Lord.

And this shall be a sign; Ye shall find the babe wrapped in swaddling clothes, lying in a manger."

And suddenly there was with the Angel a multitude of the heavenly host praising God.

When the Angels were gone, the shepherds said to one another,

"Let us go into Bethlehem to see this thing which is come to pass."

And they came with haste, and found Mary, and Joseph,
and the babe lying in a manger.

And behold, there came wise men to Jerusalem saying, "Where is He that is born King of the Jews? For we have seen His star and are come to worship Him."

And, lo, the star, which they saw in the East, went before them, till it stood over where the young child was.

When they were come into the house, they saw the young child with Mary His mother, and fell down and worshiped Him and when they had opened their treasures they presented unto Him gifts of gold, and frankincense, and myrrh.

The wise men departed into their own country and the shepherds also returned, glorifying and praising God for all the things that they had heard and seen.

And the child was called Jesus, which was so named by the Angel, before He was conceived in the womb.

For Luis

Illustrations copyright © 1986 by Julie Vivas
First published in Australia by Omnibus Books, Adelaide

All rights reserved. No part of this publication may be reproduced or transmitted in any form or by any means, electronic or mechanical, including photocopy, recording, or any information storage and retrieval system, without permission in writing from the publisher.

For information about permission to reproduce selections from this book, write to trade.permissions@hmhco.com or to Permissions, Houghton

Mifflin Harcourt Publishing Company, 3 Park Avenue, 19th Floor, New York, New York 10016.

www.hmhco.com

First U.S. edition 1988
First Voyager Books edition 1994
Restored edition 2005
Restored Voyager Books edition 2006

Voyager Books is a trademark of Harcourt, Inc., registered in the United States of America and/or other jurisdictions.

The Library of Congress has cataloged the hardcover edition as follows:
The Nativity/illustrated by Julie Vivas.
Text consists of excerpts from the authorized King James version of the Bible.
Summary: Illustrates the story of the birth of Jesus and the arrival of the wise men and shepherds at the manger.
1. Jesus Christ—Nativity—Juvenile literature. [1. Jesus Christ—Nativity. 2. Bible. N.T. Luke.]
1. Vivas, Julie, 1947– ill.
BT315.A3 1988 232.9/2 19 2005280835
ISBN-13: 978-0-15-205591-2 ISBN-10: 0-15-205591-6
ISBN-13: 978-0-15-206085-5 pb ISBN-10: 0-15-206085-5 pb

LEO 10 9
4500647499

The text type was set in Requiem.
Color separations by Bright Arts Ltd., Hong Kong
Printed and bound by LEO, China
Production supervision by Ginger Boyer
Designed by Jessica Dacher and Scott Piehl

With thanks to Ron Lander for his assistance with the selection of the text for *The Nativity.* —J.V.